The Berenstain Bears GO ON A GHOST WALK

Nothing makes a grownup bear
feel more like a cub
than ghosts and monsters
and lots of Halloween hub-bub.

WHOOOOOOOOOOOOOOOOO

The Berenstain Bears GO ON A GHOST WALK

Stan & Jan Berenstain

HarperFestival®
A Division of HarperCollins*Publishers*

The Berenstain Bears Go on a Ghost Walk
 For information address HarperCollins Children's Books, a division of HarperCollins Publishers, 10 East 53rd Street, New York, NY 10022.
www.harperchildrens.com
Library of Congress catalog card number: 2004027530
14 15 16 SCP 10 9 8 7
❖
First Edition

Papa Bear always loved Halloween.

He loved going trick-or-treating when he was a cub.

He also loved going on haunted hayrides when he was a teen.

He loved giving out treats to trick-or-treaters who came to the tree house.

But this Halloween was going to be the best yet, because he was in charge of Bear Country School's Ghost Walk. "Yessir," he said. "I'm going to put on the best Ghost Walk ever!"

"May we help?" asked Brother and Sister Bear.

"Absolutely," said Papa. "I'm going to need all the help I can get, because this is going to be the spookiest Ghost Walk in the history of Bear Country."

"Now, dear," said Mama Bear. "I know the Ghost Walk is for a good cause . . ."

"That's right," said Papa. "It's for the benefit of Bear Country School, and every cent from ticket sales is going to the school."

"That's all very well, dear," said Mama, "but I do hope you're not letting yourself get carried away."

"My dear," said Papa, "that's what Halloween is all about—getting carried away! Come, cubs. We're going to the party goods store for supplies. And afterward we're going to stop off at Farmer Ben's pumpkin patch. Ben's donating some pumpkins for the Ghost Walk."

With Halloween coming soon, the party goods store had everything Papa needed. "Let's see now," he said, "ghosts, skeletons, bats, black cats, cobwebs, scary masks, and spooky tapes to play on the school's loudspeaker system." Then, turning to the store clerk, he added, "Do you have a nice big spray can of cobwebs?"

"Just this large, economy size, sir," she said.

"That'll be fine," said Papa. "We have a whole school to cobweb."

Farmer Ben's pumpkin patch was in all its orange glory in the afternoon sun. "Greetings, Papa Bear," said Farmer Ben. "I put aside some of my best-looking pumpkins for the school Ghost Walk."

"I appreciate that, Ben," said Papa, "but good-looking pumpkins aren't what I had in mind. Don't you have any weird misshapen ones?"

"Sure," said Ben. "Over here behind the barn. I was going to grind 'em up for the hogs."

"Perfect," said Papa. "They're the ones that make the spookiest jack-o'-lanterns."

Papa went right to work on the jack-o'-lanterns when he got back to his shop. Just scooping out the insides was a lot of work. He soon had a whole trash can full of pumpkin innards.

“Spooky enough for you?” said Papa as he finished the first couple of jack-o’-lanterns.

“P-p-plenty spooky,” said Brother.

“Y-y-yes,” said Sister.

“But not as spooky as the Pumpkin Monster!” cried Papa, scooping up great gobs of gloppy innards and running after the cubs.

“Help!” they cried.

They bumped into Mama who came to see what was going on. "Please, Papa!" she said. "What are you trying to do—give the cubs nightmares?"

"It's all in fun," said Papa.

"Maybe so," said Mama, "but try to remember: One person's fun is another person's nightmare."

"But, Mama," said Papa, "Halloween is *supposed* to be scary."

"Come, cubs," said Mama. "Back to the house. It's time to start turning in."

"Gee whiz," said Papa as he headed back to his shop. "Nobody wants to have fun anymore. Everything's got to be nicey-nice, goody-two-shoes. Well, I'll show 'em."

"Whoo!" said an owl that was perched atop the shop.

"Me, Papa Q. Bear, that's who," Papa said and went back to work on his jack-o'-lanterns.

With just a few days to go until Halloween, Papa and the cubs went to work getting Bear Country School ready for the Ghost Walk.

They put Papa's super-spooky jack-o'-lanterns in every classroom.

They hung skeletons, bats, ghosts, and black cats in the corridors.

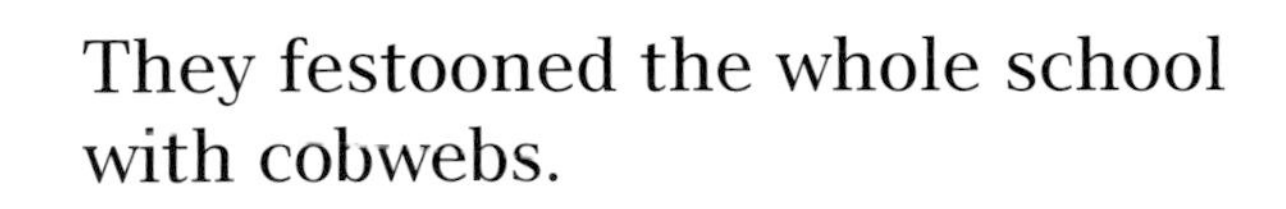

They festooned the whole school
with cobwebs.

Since this was a school Ghost Walk, Papa thought it would be a nice idea to include the great monsters of bear literature. Using masks and old clothes stuffed with straw, they made the Frankenbear Monster and Grizzula, the Bear Vampire. Then they borrowed some Ace bandages from Coach Grizzmeyer and made a bear mummy.

"Are we done, Papa?" asked Sister.

"There's just one more thing and we'll be ready for the Ghost Walk," he said.

"I want to try this spooky laughter tape on the school's loudspeaker system." Then he started the tape and the whole school was echoing with spooky laughter.

Soon it was the night before the big Ghost Walk. Brother and Sister were trying on their costumes. Brother was going to be Super Bear. Sister was going to be a princess. Baby Honey was going to be an angel. Mama decided to just wear a mask.

"Papa's going to be in charge of the whole thing," said Brother. "What's he going to be?"

"You'll see in a minute," said Mama. "He's in the other room, changing."

"Blackbear the Pirate!" cried Papa leaping into the room. "The meanest, scariest, blood-thirstiest pirate ever to sail the seas!" And was he ever! He had a hook on one hand, a dagger stuck through his skull-and-crossbones hat, and a big sword dripping blood, stuck through his chest.

Brother and Sister were terrified. Baby Honey began to cry.

"Papa!" said Mama. "How could you? Don't you remember what I said about one person's fun being another person's nightmare?"

"But, dear," said Papa, "they're not real. They're just a trick hook and dagger, and a trick sword with fake blood. See?"

He took them off and showed how they worked. "It's just for Halloween. There's nothing to be afraid of. It's all in fun."

Maybe so. But that night all of Papa's Halloween fun came to life in the scariest nightmare he ever had. The hideous gloppy pumpkin monster; the scary skeleton; bats and the black cat; the creepy ghost; the Frankenbear Monster; Grizzula, the Bear Vampire; and the Ace bandage mummy all came after him.

Terrified, Papa threw off the covers and leaped out of bed screaming, “YI-E-E-E!”

Brother and Sister came running. They and Mama comforted Papa and tried to calm him down. "I th-th-think I see what you mean about fun and nightmares," he said.

The Bear Country School Ghost Walk was a great success and a fine spooky time was had by all—even Blackbear the Pirate. He kept his trick hook, but he left his trick dagger and his trick sword with the fake blood at home.